Emma Thomson's
felicity Wishes ®

Newspaper Nerves

and other stories

Hodder
Children's
Books

A division of Hodder Headline Limited

How to make your felicity Wishes

WISH

With this book comes an extra special wish for you and your best friend.

Hold the book together at each end and both close your eyes.

Wriggle your noses and think of a number under ten.

Open your eyes, whisper the numbers you thought of to each other.

Add these numbers together. This is your

☆ Magic Number ☆

you

best friend

place your little finger on the stars, and say your magic number out loud together. Now make your wish quietly to yourselves. And maybe, one day, your wish might just come true. Love

felicity

x

For Chloe Bell and Bertie Dishes!
E.V.T

FELICITY WISHES
Felicity Wishes © 2000 Emma Thomson
Licensed by White Lion Publishing

Text and Illustrations © 2004 Emma Thomson

First published in Great Britain in 2004 by Hodder Children's Books

A Catalogue record for this book is available from the British Library

ISBN 0 340 88240 9

Printed and bound in China by Imago

The paper and board used in this paperback by Hodder Children's Books are natural recyclable
products made from wood grown in sustainable forests. The manufacturing processes
conform to the environmental regulations of the country of origin.

Hodder Children's Books
A division of Hodder Headline Ltd, 338 Euston Road, London NW1 3BH

CONTENTS

Felicity Wishes flew with heavy wings towards school. It was Monday morning. Monday had become Felicity's least favourite day since the start of the new term. Each week began with an extra long class of double Magic Maths.

"If only we could start the week with something more fun, like cooking," sighed Felicity as she led the way out of assembly with her friends, Holly, Polly and Daisy.

"I can't understand why you don't like it. Maths really is magic!" said Polly, who was the cleverest of all the fairy friends by far.

"There's only one thing magic about maths, and that's how every minute in the class feels like an hour!" giggled Felicity, stopping to look at the school notice board.

Felicity, Holly, Polly and Daisy all went to the School of Nine Wishes. One day they would graduate to become proper fairies with a beautiful pair of double wings.

"Hey! Look at this!" said Holly, pointing to a poster. "It may be just the thing to help you have a happy Monday morning, Felicity!"

Felicity was gone in a flutter leaving Polly, Daisy and Holly to go to Magic Maths without her. When she met up with them at break time she could hardly contain her excitement!

"It's fantastic, there are going to be sections in the paper on everything you can possibly think of: fashion, wishes, dreams, magic, shopping … all the things that we love!" said Felicity, bouncing up and down and clapping her hands. "Fairy Godmother wants a team of fairies to put it together, to do everything from photography to reporting. She even needs one fairy to be a Fashion Editor."

Holly's eyes lit up. "How is Fairy Godmother going to choose who does what?" she asked, already imagining herself with a notebook and pen, commenting on the fairy fashions of the day.

"Well, each fairy who wants to be considered should fill in one of these," said Felicity, rummaging around her bag and producing four application forms, "and hand it in with an example of their work by the end of next week. The fairies chosen will get their efforts printed in the first ever issue."

School Newspaper
Nine Wish Weekly

APPLICATION FORM

Name ....

House ....

Would like to apply for the position of: (tick one box)

1. Senior Editor ☐   4. Advertising Manager ☐

2. Fashion Editor ☐   5. Art Editor ☐

3. Photographer ☐   6. Senior Reporter ☐

Signed ....

Over the next few days the fairies could think of nothing else. Holly, who wanted to be a Christmas Tree Fairy when she graduated from the School of Nine Wishes, had already decided that nothing but the position of Fashion Editor would fulfil her truest potential.

Polly thought that she'd be most suited to Advertising Manager. She was always very organised.

Daisy didn't mind what she did as long as it was to do with flowers, but after quickly scanning the list she'd noted there wasn't a Flower Editor. Instead she'd settled on setting her sights on the position of Senior Reporter. That way she could add a flowery angle to everything she wrote about.

Poor Felicity. Her friends had chosen to apply for all the jobs she thought she'd be good at and she didn't want to ruin their chances by competing against them.

"What about Photographer?" said Holly, feeling bad.

"I dropped my camera," said Felicity.

"Well, we can probably mend it," volunteered Polly.

"You'll have to find it first," said Felicity, looking down at her toes. "I was flying above Little Blossoming at the time!"

"What about Art Editor then?" said Polly.

"I'm terrible at drawing," said Felicity. "Even my stick fairies look bad." Felicity opened up her homework book to show her friends her disastrous attempts.

"Don't worry," Felicity said, feeling bad about her friends' concern. "I can help you all with your articles and see if I get any ideas along the way. I think we should start with some research right now!"

Felicity, Holly, Polly and Daisy skipped off towards Sparkles, their favourite café on the corner.

* * *

When Daisy handed Felicity her article to read, two days later, it was bound in the most beautiful file covered with a delicate pattern of real flower petals.

"Wow," gasped Felicity, almost too afraid to hold it.

"There's a petal from every flower in my garden," said Daisy proudly. As Felicity opened the first page, she continued, "And each page has a drawing of every leaf."

"That's beautiful," said Felicity in awe, turning the precious pages one by one. When she reached the end

she looked up at
Daisy, confused.
"Where are the
words?" she
asked.

"Oh," replied
Daisy, "do you
think it needs words? I thought the
beauty of the flowers spoke for
themselves."

Not wishing to hurt her friend's
feelings, Felicity agreed. "Oh, they
do, they do. You couldn't put into
words how lovely they are. But…"
and Felicity thought carefully before
she spoke, "…a story about your
flowers could help enhance their
beauty, and make it more interesting
for people to read."

"Yes, I see what you mean," said
Daisy, patting the front cover of her
file gently.

"Why don't we fly to Roots 'n'

Shoots, to find some inspiration for a story?" suggested Felicity. And Daisy, who never needed an excuse to visit a garden centre, readily agreed.

* * *

When they got there they found it was closed. A glum-looking fairy was locking up the front gate just as they landed.

"I don't understand," said Daisy as she approached the fairy, whose badge told them her name was Sorrell. "Today's not your usual day for half day closing."

"I'm afraid we've only been open for half a day every day this week," Sorrell replied, slipping the key into her pocket and looking as though she was about to cry.

"But why?" asked Daisy. "Have you run out of flowers?"

"If only!" said Sorrell. "A large new out of town shopping centre has opened with a gardening shop that's much easier to fly to. We just don't have the customers to stay open all day any more."

"That's terrible," said Felicity.

"If only there was something we could do," said Daisy, sighing.

"There is!" said Felicity, having a brain-wave. "Wait here both of you!" and in a flutter she was off.

* * *

Sorrell and Daisy were deep in conversation when Felicity arrived back with Polly and Holly.

Polly sat down with a professional air opposite the two fairies. "Felicity explained on the way here that you need some help reminding people where Roots 'n' Shoots is." She got out her notebook and pen.

"An advertisement in *Nine Wish Weekly* would be perfect!"

"Yes, I think that might help," said Sorrell. "I was just telling Daisy all about it. It's almost as if our lovely garden centre doesn't exist."

"It soon won't," said Daisy, "if the out of town centre takes much more of your business."

"What you need is something big and bold," said Polly.

"With an article in the press to let everyone know what's been happening!" said Felicity, nudging Daisy.

Not to be outdone, Holly joined in, "and I can do a makeover for Sorrell, with before and after shots. I really think with your gorgeous long hair, Sorrell, we can try some really exciting styles!"

"Perhaps you could show how to use this season's colours for a fashionable look at work," suggested Felicity.

"That's a great idea, Felicity," replied Holly. "Thank you!"

Felicity was delighted that all her friends had come up with such great ideas, but she couldn't help wondering if there was anything she could do. For now she'd just have to make do with making useful suggestions.

The School of Nine Wishes was full of excitement. All the fairies who wanted to work on the *Nine Wish Weekly* had finished their pieces, filled in their forms and were standing in line to hand them in to Fairy Godmother.

"There are so many fairies applying," said Holly, with a concerned edge to her voice.

"Look at the pile for photographer," said Polly, pointing at the growing pile on Fairy Godmother's desk.

"I'm glad I did drop my camera!" said Felicity. " I'd never have stood a chance."

"I'm not sure any of us do," said Polly, who had quickly added up all the people in the queue and done her sums.

* * *

It was several days later. The friends had almost forgotten about their newspaper applications when a very loud fairy burst into Sparkles with such a noise that Felicity nearly dropped her milkshake.

"I've done it! I've got the job of Reporter!" she announced to all her friends. "Fairy Godmother just put up the list on the notice board." She plonked herself next to a timid-looking fairy dressed entirely in green. "I can't be sure but I think you have been chosen as Fashion Editor."

Felicity and her friends looked on in amazement. "Well, that's that," said Holly, tears welling up in her eyes. "All those wasted hair dos!"

"Hair dos?" said Daisy, dismayed. 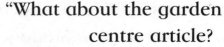 "What about the garden centre article?

ı't get printed if I haven't been ı, and that might mean the end of Roots 'n' Shoots for ever." Everyone looked forlorn.

"Not necessarily," said Felicity, who pointed out that they still didn't know who had been chosen as Advertising Manager.

"The advert could still save the garden cen—" But before Polly could finish her sentence there was a large whoop of "Hurray" on the other table of fairies and one with very long hair stood up to allow herself to be heard.

"Hot chocolates for everyone are on me!" she said, addressing the whole café. "I've just been made Advertising Manager on the *Nine Wish Weekly*."

Silently Felicity, Holly, Polly and Daisy slowly pulled on their coats and got up to leave. None of them felt much like hot chocolate. Felicity was almost glad she hadn't applied for any of the jobs.

* * *

When the fairy friends all met the next morning to fly to school together everyone was still very quiet. Felicity felt sad just because her friends were. It was worse than any other Monday morning.

Fairy Godmother and four beaming fairy helpers were handing out the first edition of the *Nine Wish Weekly* to everyone arriving.

Felicity, Holly, Polly and Daisy solemnly took a copy each.

"Cheer up, girls," Fairy Godmother chirped. "I thought you four, of all the fairies in the school, would be happy today."

Felicity and her friends stopped and looked up.

"It's not every day you get your first newspaper contribution in print!" she said, ruffling Felicity's hair with her wand. "I'm very proud of you all, you make a great team." She beamed at the fairies. "Without you, Felicity, it couldn't have happened, which is why I've made you Senior Editor."

"Senior Editor?" said Felicity, confused.

"You did see the list?" said Fairy Godmother, untangling her wand and pointing to the notice board.

Daisy unfolded her newspaper and couldn't believe her eyes. There in black and white was the article she'd written about saving Roots 'n' Shoots on the front page!

Frantically, Holly leafed through the pages of her copy before she squealed, "My fairy makeover! Look!"

"Fairy Godmother," said Polly, still not quite understanding, "there was a fairy in Sparkles that was Fashion Editor, and another that was celebrating being Advertising Manager..."

"There were so many great applicants we have increased the size of the team. They are your juniors!" said Fairy Godmother. "I'm glad you've met already. I hope they'll be a great help to you. The first meeting's today at lunch time. See you then!" and she was gone in a twinkle.

None of the fairy friends could quite believe what they had just heard.

"Well," said Felicity, beaming, "if we're going to be writing a newspaper then this is the last time we're not the first to hear the latest gossip!"

Helping friends...

...helps you to shine

Magical Mysteries

"Are you *sure* it
doesn't look silly?"
said Felicity Wishes,
parading up and down in front of
her friends, wearing her disguise.

"No one will ever know it's you,"
said Polly, giggling uncontrollably.

"They will if they see your stripy
tights," said Holly, pointing. Felicity
always wore stripy tights. Most other
fashion conscious fairies had
stopped wearing them ages ago, but
Felicity was adamant that they were
a "classic" and had a wardrobe full
of them.

"Here," said Daisy, rummaging around in her bag. "I've got a spare pair of spotty ones, you can borrow mine."

Felicity and her three fairy friends, Holly, Polly and Daisy, all went to the School of Nine Wishes where they had just been put in charge of running the school newspaper, the *Nine Wish Weekly*. Stuck for stories to write, Felicity had volunteered to go undercover in order to find a scoop for the next edition.

"Right," said Polly, taking charge, "Let's get you in position," and they all headed off to Sparkles, the café on the corner.

Since the café was the place that most fairies went after school to enjoy a gossip, Felicity and her friends had decided it would be the best place to start to find a good story.

"Testing, testing," Felicity whispered

huskily under her breath into the microphone hidden secretly under her raincoat collar.

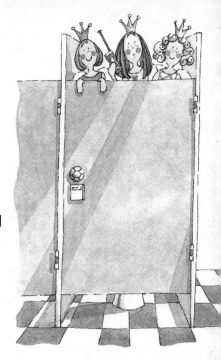

"Roger, receiving you loud and clear," said Holly. All three fairy friends were squidged into the last cubicle in the toilets, with note-books poised.

"Oooo, how exciting!" said Polly a little too loudly.

"Shhh," whispered Holly. "We don't want our cover blown. If people know we're in here eavesdropping on their gossip, no one will say anything."

Polly raised her eyebrows as if to say sorry, and pretended to zip up her mouth.

Holly gave her the thumbs-up in return, and they waited, wings quivering in anticipation.

"Two strange-looking fairies in sunglasses have just come into the café and sat down," crackled Felicity's voice through the receiver. "They're both carrying very large suitcases," she continued. "They look to me like they could be running away."

"That would be a great story!" hissed Holly into her microphone.

"Try to overhear why they'd want to leave Little Blossoming."

"Roger," came the reply, and for a few moments everything was silent. Holly, Polly and Daisy took the opportunity to scribble notes in their reporters' pads.

"One of them just said they'll have to be quick, because they have to leave soon." Felicity's voice was hushed over the receiver. "They must have done something very bad if they need to leave in a rush. Over and out."

"What are they wearing?" said Holly, always aware of the fashion angle for her readers. "Do they have 'bad' clothes?"

Felicity made no response.

"I wonder why she won't answer," whispered Holly, tapping the receiver. "Felicity... Felicity? Come in..."

"Oh goodness!" said Polly too loudly

again, her mind working overtime.
"What if the bad fairies have got
Felicity!"

Dropping their notebooks and
abandoning their listening
equipment, Holly,
Polly and Daisy
fell over each
other to spring
from the
cubicle and
burst out
into the
café.

Felicity was nowhere to be seen!

"Gracious!" said Daisy. "They've
got her. They must have found out
that Felicity was listening to their
conversation and knew they were
planning on running away, and
they've kidnapped her!"

"What shall we do?" said Polly, a
little scared.

"Find her!" said Holly, dashing towards the door. "Come on, let's go!"

All three fairy friends ran out of the café and stood puffing, out of breath, on the corner of Star Street, scanning the crowds of shopping fairies frantically for a glimpse of their friend.

Just then, a familiar voice spoke to them from behind.

"What are you doing here? I thought you were supposed to be in the toilets?" said Felicity, confused.

"What are you doing here?" said Polly, almost in tears. "We thought you'd been kidnapped by the bad fairies."

"Oh, they weren't bad fairies at all in the end. In fact they were lovely. I've just helped them carry their suitcases to the bus stop. They're going on holiday to Fairy World. Lucky them…" mused Felicity.

"No front page scoop, then!" said Holly, feeling a bit silly.

"At least we don't have to rescue you!" said Daisy, turning to head back to Sparkles. "Perhaps we should give up on spying for the day and have a hot chocolate instead!"

* * *

After all the mornings excitement, Felicity decided to be lazy and treat herself to the bus home. She was lucky; even though the bus was busy there was just one seat left.

"Floella!" said Felicity, recognising the fairy as she sat down next to her.

"Hello, Felicity!" said Floella, moving all her heavy bags out of the way.

"What a lot of shopping!" Felicity remarked.

"I've been doing a favour for someone," said Floella, looking awkward. "There's not much else for a Frost Fairy to do at this time of year."

"Hmm, I suppose not," said Felicity, who couldn't help but notice that the bags were full of all of her favourite things: crisps, sweeties, balloons and streamers.

"Is your friend having a party?" she asked curiously.

Floella suddenly went very red. "Erm… I don't know… I think this is my stop…" And she hastily gathered up all her bags. "See you soon, Felicity!" and, in a flutter, Floella was gone.

"How strange," thought Felicity as the bus continued on its journey. "That wasn't Floella's stop at all. I'm sure she lives much further up the hill."

✳ ✳ ✳

A few days passed before Holly, Polly, Daisy and Felicity all met up again.

"We still don't have anything exciting for our front page," moaned Holly, flicking through her notebook.

"Fairy Godmother was seen wearing odd socks the other day," said Polly, scanning her list.

"That's not a story," said Felicity giggling. "I don't think many fairies would be clamouring for a copy! I can just see it now," she said, looking up dreamily, "'Silly Sock Mix-up for Fairy in charge'."

"No, I suppose you're right," said Polly, a little put out. "But you must admit, it's very unlike Fairy Godmother. Perhaps she's been a bit busy recently."

"Ahhh," said Holly, getting excited. "Busy doing what? That's the sort of question a professional reporter asks."

Suddenly Daisy, who'd been absentmindedly doodling flower pictures, sprang to life. "Maybe Fairy Godmother has something to do with what's going on at Nine Wish Wood!"

"What do you mean?" said Felicity, the others staring open-mouthed.

"I'm not sure," said Daisy. "I go there quite often to keep an eye on the flowers, tend to the broken ones and water any that have escaped the rain. But the last few times I've been I've noticed something very strange..."

Holly, Polly and Felicity shuffled forward on their seats and leaned forward.

"...More than the average number of fairy footprints. I'm not the only one who's been visiting Nine Wish Wood."

"Let's not jump to conclusions,"
said Polly, sitting up sensibly.
"Remember last week and the bad
fairies, who just turned out to be
going on holiday?"

"Yes," agreed Holly. "You're right,
more footprints means nothing,
probably just some friends on a
nature trail or something."

"Well," said Daisy, who'd gone back to her doodling, "that would certainly explain the footprints, but it wouldn't explain the FOUR... BIG... HOLES!"

Suddenly the fairy friends were all of a flutter and within minutes they were winging their way to Nine Wish Wood.

"It's so mysterious," said Holly, twiddling her wand and looking deep into the blackness below.

"There's only one way I think we can solve this mystery," called out Felicity, her toes teetering on the edge of one of the other holes. "I think if we find out who's been leaving the footprints then we'll see who made the holes. All we have to do is watch and wait."

Everyone agreed it was a good plan and, without wasting any time, Daisy found hiding places, while Holly and Polly flew off to make a packed lunch that would last them throughout the night if needed.

* * *

By late afternoon all the fairies were in position and anxiously watching for signs of movement.

Dusk fell, and the wood became colder and more shadowy.

More time passed.

Felicity reached into the bag and pulled out the last jam sandwich.

"Anyone mind if I have this?" she asked politely.

"Go ahead," said Daisy, who had been dozing quietly in the arms of a large oak tree.

"Don't rustle the bag so much, we don't want to give away our hiding places," said Holly sharply.

"I'm not rustling the bag!" whispered Felicity and she popped the last bite into her mouth.

"Then what's that noise?" said Polly.

"LOOK!" hissed Daisy from her lookout. "There's a light!"

Silently all the fairy friends peered over into the semi-darkness to where Daisy was pointing, and saw to their amazement a huge white figure, lit with an eerie glow, heading towards them.

"It's a ghost!" whispered Polly under her breath.

"It's got fairies
all around it!" said Holly,
squinting as it loomed nearer.
"This is going to make a great story."

"It's getting bigger!" gasped Daisy,
terrified.

"Arghh!" screamed Felicity at the
top of her voice, giving away their
hiding place.

"What are you fairies doing?"
boomed a voice from behind
the white figure,
which was now
standing in
front of
them.

Daisy nearly fell out of her tree
with fright.

"We j-j-j-j-just wanted to g-g-get a
f-f-f-front p-p-p-page story for our
s-s-s-school p-p-p-paper," she stuttered
shakily, hanging on to a branch.

"It was supposed to be a surprise,"
said the voice which sounded strangely
familiar, "but seeing as you're here
you can all give us a hand."

"FAIRY GODMOTHER!"
the friends chorused,
as she emerged
from behind the
white shape.

"I don't know
why you're
so surprised,"
she said,
flying closer
to them.
"I'm the only
one who can

give permission for a party to be held in Nine Wish Wood."

"A party?" frowned Felicity.

Just then, they all realised what Fairy Godmother was saying. As their eyes grew more accustomed to the lamplight they could see it wasn't a ghost at all. It was a large white marquee! Fairies all around were helping to lift it into position,

on top of four large posts that had been placed in four very deep holes.

"Yes, it's a surprise midsummer party to be held tomorrow night for all the fairies in Little Blossoming. Everything has to be set up this evening in good time."

"So, no mystery, no ghost, and no story for the *Nine Wish Weekly* front cover again," sighed Felicity, who was upset at seeing the disappointment in all her friends' faces. And then she had an idea.

"Fairy Godmother," said Felicity, "everyone has put in so much effort behind the scenes to keep this party a secret," and she looked towards dozens of busy fairies who were preparing food, decorating tables and blowing up balloons. "Wouldn't it be wonderful if the *Nine Wish Weekly* did an exclusive article?"

"What a fantastic idea, Felicity,"

said Fairy Godmother, trying to
contain her own excitement. "The
front page could read 'Secret
Midsummer Party Surprises All!'"
And everyone cheered.

"Save me a copy!" Fairy Godmother called as she flew off to help the preparations, but Felicity's friends were so hugging her so tightly she didn't hear!

FREE

Nine Wish
WEEKLY

Secret Midsummer Party Surprises All!

By Felicity Wishes

On Midsummer's day, a group of fairy reporters discovered more than the average number of fairy footprints in Nine Wish Wood. This find started one of the most interesting investigations in Little Blossoming for years.

(Continued on page 4)

friends together

help scary
situations disappear

Dessert Disaster

"Late again?" whispered Holly to
Felicity Wishes, as she skidded to a
halt next to her in the assembly line.

"I can't go anywhere without
fairies wanting to stop and talk to
me!" said Felicity under her breath.
"I had to stop six times on the way
into school this morning. Has it been
the same for you?"

"Worse!" said Holly. "I got up early
especially, and even then I just got
here within a whisper of nine
o'clock."

Felicity and her friends, Holly, Polly and Daisy, had become well known in the town of Little Blossoming since they had begun working on the school newspaper, the *Nine Wish Weekly*. The last edition, which featured the Surprise Midsummer Party, had distributed more copies than ever before.

"I've never been so popular," Holly continued, as she took her seat in the school hall.

"I don't think there's a fairy in Little Blossoming who doesn't want to be on the front page of the paper with some story or other," said Felicity, a little downhearted. "If only we had enough room for them all."

"Uh-oh," said Holly, spotting Miss Meandering the geography teacher heading towards them. "Looks like we're going to get told off for talking."

"Fairies!" burst out Miss Meandering.

"Sorry, Miss," said Felicity and Holly at the same time.

"Sorry?" said Miss Meandering, looking quizzical. "You've nothing to be sorry for. I've just come to ask you both if you'd like to come and see my rock collection at lunch time. I think it would make an absolutely super centre fold spread for the paper. And perhaps..." she looked a little coy, "...you'd consider a close-up of me with my favourite rock for the front page?"

Holly tried to contain her giggles, and let Felicity reply politely, "The stories for the next issue have already been written, I'm afraid, Miss Meandering. Maybe we could see your lovely rock collection another time."

And to make sure Miss Meandering didn't feel too bad, Felicity added, "It sounds like it would make a lovely feature though."

"Yes, yes," said Miss Meandering, trying hard not to show her disappointment. "A 'feature', yes that does sound good." And she bustled off just as Fairy Godmother began to read her notices for the day ahead.

* * *

When Holly, Polly, Daisy and Felicity all met up at break time no one appeared very happy.

"I feel so terrible," began Felicity. "So many fairies have so many wonderful stories. If only there was a way we could print them all."

"I know," agreed Daisy. "Some fairies have really good causes they want to draw attention too, like the Poorly Fairy Fund."

"We already have more stories than we can print this week," said Holly, scanning her reporter's note pad.

"I've got something that will cheer us all up," said Polly, producing a gold envelope from her school bag. "It's a personal invitation for the school newspaper team from Jenny Olivia, the famous celebrity chef, to a private pre-opening meal at her new restaurant!"

"WOW!" said Holly, licking her lips. "Her fairy cakes are the lightest I've ever tasted."

"You've been to one of her restaurants before?" asked Felicity in awe.

"No, no, someone gave me her

latest cookery book as a present last year."

"There will be so many famous fairies there!" said Holly, swishing her hair dramatically. "Just think of the photos we'll be able to take for the paper."

"Whatever will I wear?" said Felicity, already fretting about the most important question.

* * *

At last the day arrived when all four of the fairies would sample the delights from a professional fairy kitchen. Even though she wasn't very good at it, Felicity loved cooking and she had already telephoned to arrange an interview with all the kitchen staff, for their top tips, at the end of the night. Holly, Polly, Daisy and Felicity could barely keep their crowns on with excitement.

A long pink limo arrived at
Felicity's house to collect them all
just as the clock struck eight. Lying

back against the soft rose velvet interior, they poured themselves delicate tall glasses of raspberry lemonade.

"This is the life!" said Holly, taking her first sip with her eyes closed.

"There are ups and downs with running the school paper," said Polly, thinking of the late nights spent writing articles. "And being invited out on evenings like this is definitely one of the ups!"

When they arrived, two prim-looking fairies, dressed in elegant black and white stripy dresses, held large glass doors open on to a room that glowed with golden light.

All four fairies stood open-mouthed.

"We mustn't forget we're here to take notes and photos for the paper," said Felicity, who could have quite happily stood there open-mouthed for the whole evening!

Famous celebrity fairies hovered gracefully around the room where tables were positioned at different heights, suspended by shimmering silver cords. Tiny fairy lights dusted with a pale pink sparkly powder lit the eating area with a twinkly glow.

"Isn't this magical?" said Daisy.

"Beautiful," breathed Felicity, who had butterflies in her tummy.

"Have you seen Stella Fluttiano over there?" said Holly excitedly, trying not to point. Stella Fluttiano was the designer fairy whose style all fashion-conscious fairies followed.

"Just look at that outfit! If only Fairy Godmother would let us dress like that in class!"

"Forget about Stella Fluttiano," said Polly, bouncing up and down excitedly. "Look who's sitting at the best table, Natasha Milletova!" and all the fairies' eyes turned to rest on the great prima ballerina.

At the sound of a soft silver gong everyone took their seats and Jenny Olivia stood to make a speech.

"Fairies, thank you for joining me this evening for this very special night. This is the preview night where all my friends and associates can sample the dishes on my new menu before the public. Members of the press, I ask you to be kind, as your reviews could make or break the success of this venture. It is a project into which I have put my whole heart, and one that I am extremely proud of. Have a lovely evening and bon appetit."

The whole room raised their glasses and cheered as a dozen waitresses flew into the room holding ten delicately balanced plates on each arm.

The food was truly delicious.

Chez Olivia
MENU

Starter
Star spangled midnight soup with tiny frosted magic croutons

Main course
Layered secret rainbow parcels with wand warmed vegetables

Pudding
Frothy surprise with jewel fruits and flutter ribbons of chocolate

Felicity and her friends were more than happy not to be flying home that night, their tummies were so full. Instead they fell into the same pink limo that had brought them and dozed their way home.

* * *

The next day, Holly, Polly and Felicity met under the large oak tree at break time for a quick newspaper meeting. If the article on the restaurant was to make the next issue, it had to be written by the following day.

"Where's Daisy?" said Felicity. "I couldn't find her in morning assembly."

"She's poorly," said Holly, reaching into her bag for her break-time Sparkle Bar. "When I called round her house on the way into school she was still in bed. Her tummy is making the most bubbly rumblings I've ever heard!"

"Poor Daisy," said Felicity, who cared deeply about all her friends. "I'll go round and see her on the way home, and take her some flowers to cheer her up."

"I have to say," said Holly, "I'm not feeling great. Anyone want my Sparkle Bar? I don't really fancy it."

"That's a first!" said Polly. "You not wanting chocolate! I hope whatever you're feeling isn't catching!"

"Has everyone got their notes and photos from last night?" asked Felicity, whose job it was to get everything ready for the printers. "I'll finish writing about our wonderful restaurant experience when I get home from school, and we should be able to have it on the front page for the paper's next issue."

"Jenny Olivia will be so pleased to have a lovely review," said Polly.

"Her restaurant certainly deserved it," said Holly. "I've never had such a lovely m—" Holly was going to say "meal" but her tummy, which made the most enormous bubbly rumble, drowned her out! Holly quickly flew off.

"Oh dear," said Felicity, flying after Holly. "I'll go and see that she's all right. Meet you here again at lunch time."

* * *

When lunch time came, Felicity had some bad news for Polly. Holly was poorly too and had gone home to rest in bed.

"Looks like there's only you and me left to write about the restaurant, Pol."

"Actually," said Polly, holding her tummy with one hand and covering her mouth with the other, "it might only be you, I'm afraid. All through Chemistry my tummy was rumbling so much that Miss Sparkle thought it was one of my experiments that had gone wrong! When she found out it was my bubbly belly she sent me to the nurse who has given me permission to take the afternoon off classes." Right on cue Polly's tummy

made a dramatic bubbly rumbling sound that could be heard on the other side of the field!

"I'll fly home with you now," said Felicity, concerned. "You shouldn't fly home alone if you're feeling poorly."

As Felicity flew back to school, after carefully tucking Polly up in bed, she asked herself something she had hardly dared to think.

"I wonder if all these bubbly

tummies are anything to do with the food from Jenny Olivia's kitchen? If they are," she thought to herself, "I'm not sure that it would be very honest to write a good review for the school paper."

Felicity just didn't know what to do. After all the hard work Jenny Olivia had put into the restaurant, and the wonderful night they had all had, she really wanted it to be a success for her. The last thing she wanted to do was write a bad review, but she didn't want to lie either.

* * *

The afternoon passed slowly for Felicity. After dropping the flowers off

at Daisy's house, and popping in
briefly to see Holly, Felicity flew home
with heavy wings. She poured herself
a large strawberry milkshake and
settled down to go through the
restaurant notes and photos.

The proper thing to do, she thought,
after taking her final slurp, was to
telephone Jenny Olivia and tell her
about her three poorly fairy friends.
There might be other poorly fairies,
and if there was something wrong
with the food then Jenny Olivia could
make sure it was put right before
she opened to the public. Felicity was
just about to reluctantly pick up the

phone when she saw something that made her heart leap.

The next morning Felicity dropped off the final draft of the newspaper at the printers and flew to school. She wasn't surprised to see Holly, Polly and Daisy all looking their usual

selves standing in the queue for
assembly.

"Feeling better?" she asked as she
joined them.

"Yes, thank you, Felicity," said Daisy.
"If it hadn't have been for your visit
last night then I'm sure we'd all still
be in bed, worrying about what might
be wrong with us."

"I still don't know how you knew
what made us poorly," mused Holly.

"Let's just say, I think you got your
just desserts!" Felicity said, rummaging
in her bag and producing a print-out
of the photo for them all to see.

When the restaurant opened to the public that Saturday, queues for a table stretched as far as Star Street. Jenny Olivia was so delighted with the review that she invited the fairies back for a complimentary dinner. Strangely enough, not even Holly could be persuaded to have the chocolate pudding for dessert!

FREE

Nine Wish
WEEKLY

Olivia offers
Delicious Dining
Experience

By Felicity, Holly, Polly and Daisy

This week our roving fairy reporters were invited to Jenny Olivia's latest restaurant opening – Chez Olivia – which opened with a star studded preview evening.

Continued on page 2.

Dilemmas dissolve

if you stop and listen
to your heart

If you enjoyed this book, why not try another of these fantastic story collections?

Clutter Clean-out

Designer Drama

Newspaper Nerves

Star Surprise

Also available in the Felicity Wishes range:

Felicity Wishes: Snowflakes and Sparkledust

It is time for spring to arrive in Little Blossoming but there is a problem and winter is staying put. Can Felicity Wishes get the seasons back on track?

Felicity Wishes: Secrets and Surprises

Felicity Wishes is planning her birthday party but it seems none of her friends can come. Will Felicity end up celebrating her birthday alone?

Felicity Wishes has lots to say in these fantastic little books:

Little Book of Love

Little Book of Peace

Little Book of Hiccups

Little Book of Every Day Wishes

Little Book of Fun